ZONDERKIDZ

Whatever You Grow Up to Be
Copyright © 2014 by Karen Kingsbury
Illustrations © 2014 by Valeria Docampo

Requests for information should be addressed to:
Zonderkidz, 5300 Patterson Ave SE, Grand Rapids, Michigan 49530

Library of Congress Cataloging-in-Publication Data
Kingsbury, Karen.
       Whatever you grow up to be / by Karen Kingsbury.
           pages cm
       Summary: From birth to football games to college graduation to fatherhood, a mother reminds
   her son that life is filled with possibilities and that God has a plan for him—whatever he grows up to
   be. Bible verses are interspersed throughout the text.
       ISBN 978-0-310-71646-4
       [1. Stories in rhyme. 2. Growth—Fiction. 3. Mothers and sons—Fiction. 4. Christian life—
   Fiction.] I. Title.
   PZ8.3.K6145Wh   2014
   E—dc23   2013027575

Published in association with the literary agency of Alive Communications, Inc.,
7680 Goddard Street, Suite 200, Colorado Springs, Colorado 80920.
www.alivecommunications.com

Zonderkidz is a trademark of Zondervan.

Editor: Barbara Herndon
Art direction and design: Jody Langley

Printed in China

14 15 16 17 18 19 20/DSC/ 6 5 4 3 2 1

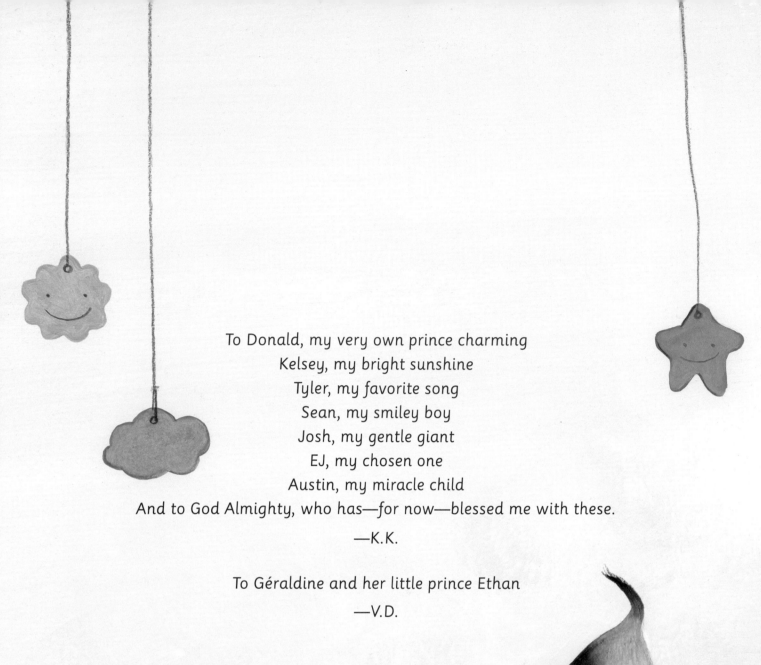

To Donald, my very own prince charming
Kelsey, my bright sunshine
Tyler, my favorite song
Sean, my smiley boy
Josh, my gentle giant
EJ, my chosen one
Austin, my miracle child
And to God Almighty, who has—for now—blessed me with these.

—K.K.

To Géraldine and her little prince Ethan

—V.D.

Whatever You Grow Up to Be

KAREN KINGSBURY

ILLUSTRATED BY VALERIA DOCAMPO

ZONDERkidz

Ten little toes right from the start
Make footprints on your mommy's heart!

His mother treasured all these things in her heart.— LUKE 2:51

You wiggle, giggle, start to crawl,
Take baby steps, and then you fall.
You try again, I hold your hand,
Then on your own you learn to stand.

God has plans, can't wait to see,
Whatever you grow up to be.

"For I know the plans I have for you," declares the LORD, "plans to prosper
you and not to harm you, plans to give you hope and a future."
—JEREMIAH 29:11

You came to greet him with rich blessings and placed a crown of pure gold upon his head.— P S A L M 2 1 : 3

And when my precious boy turns five,
I'll stay close, right by your side.
A crown upon your handsome head,
A castle fort beside your bed,
As prince you'll rule so royally,
If that's what you grow up to be.

Stand firm in the faith; be courageous; be strong.— 1 CORINTHIANS 16:13

At ten you drive your fire truck,
And rescue folks when they get stuck.
A brave, courageous hero boy,
Your daddy's pride and mama's joy.
You'll fight those fires faithfully,
If that's what you grow up to be.

Middle school and you're thirteen;
Cleats and jersey, crisp and clean.

I'll cheer you on and shout your name,
And sit front row at every game.
A football star—my MVP,
If that's what you grow up to be.

I will be glad and rejoice in you ... —PSALM 9:2

My heart, O God, is steadfast;
I will sing and make music with all my soul.— PSALM 108:1

Car keys in hand, you'll turn sixteen;
Girls and friends and rock star dreams.
You'll play guitar in your own band
And someday be a music man.
You'll sing on stage, from sea to sea,
If that's what you grow up to be.

College sees my boy take wing;
Drama, science, marketing.

Direct my footsteps according
to your word ...
—PSALM 119:133

In leadership, you'll take a stand.
My brilliant boy—a businessman.
You'll work in faith and honesty,
If that's what you grow up to be.

That is why a man leaves his father
and mother and is united to his wife,
and they become one flesh.
—GENESIS 2:24

A pretty girl, your wedding day...
I always knew you couldn't stay.
A vow, a kiss for your new wife;
It's time to start a brand-new life.
One day you'll raise a family,
If that's what you grow up to be.

Children's children are a crown to the aged ...—PROVERBS 17:6

Ten little toes,
right from the start
Make footprints on his
grandma's heart.

He wiggles, giggles, starts to crawl,
Takes baby steps, and then he falls.
He tries again, I hold his hand,
Then on his own he learns to stand.
God has plans, can't wait to see,
What that grandboy grows up to be.

"For I know the plans I have for you," declares the LORD, "plans to prosper you and not to harm you, plans to give you hope and a future."
—JEREMIAH 29:11